Praise for **Gail A**

For the Claire Abbott Mystery

"[Claire] is a relatable character, and her psychic ability grows at just the right pace for a short series opener. For new adult readers who prefer hi-lo books and reluctant or struggling teen readers."

— School Library Journal

"Black forests, snowy weather and a growing sense of dread stir the pot of fear and tension to a deadly twister resulting in drastic action, last second rescue and several red faces among the town's male protectors of the peace. A sleuth with an edge launches Claire Abbott into a new series."

—Canadian Mystery Reviews

. "A mad dash from start to finish, this latest entry in the Rapid Reads series is great for people who crave excitement."

—Kirkus Reviews

For *The Spawning Grounds*

"Writing as fluid as the river that runs through the story… A master storyteller, Anderson-Dargatz sets out with a tale of the familiar and seamlessly takes the reader where they never imagined they could go."

—The Toronto Star

"The Canadian novelist writes what's sure to be classic literature."

—The Huffington Post

"Sharp imagery and spare dialogue are put to good use in Gail Anderson-Dargatz's ghost tale of a mysterious force intent on destroying a family in rural British Columbia."

—The Globe and Mail

Praise for **Gail Anderson-Dargatz**

From Scratch

GAIL ANDERSON-DARGATZ

ORCA BOOK PUBLISHERS

Library and Archives Canada Cataloguing in Publication

Anderson-Dargatz, Gail, 1963–, author
From scratch / Gail Anderson-Dargatz.
(Rapid reads)

Issued also in print and electronic formats.
ISBN 978-1-4598-1502-5 (softcover).—ISBN 978-1-4598-1503-2 (PDF).—
ISBN 978-1-4598-1504-9 (EPUB)

I. Title. II. Series: Rapid reads
PS8551.N3574F76 2017   C813'.54   C2017-900823-4
C2017-900824-2

First published in the United States, 2017
Library of Congress Control Number: 2017933365

Summary: In this short novel, a single mother goes back to school in order
to run her own bakery. (RL 4.8)

*Orca Book Publishers is dedicated to preserving the environment and has
printed this book on Forest Stewardship Council® certified paper.*

Orca Book Publishers gratefully acknowledges the support for
its publishing programs provided by the following agencies:
the Government of Canada through the Canada Book Fund and the
Canada Council for the Arts, and the Province of British Columbia
through the BC Arts Council and the Book Publishing Tax Credit.

Cover design by Jenn Playford
Cover photography by Creative Market

ORCA BOOK PUBLISHERS
www.orcabook.com

Printed and bound in Canada.

20 19 18 17 • 4 3 2 1

For Judi, who brought a community together with her fine cooking and loving presence.

One

I brushed flour off my apron as I stepped away from the kitchen area and up to the bakery counter to serve Murray. He was a widower a few years older than me, in his early forties. He still dressed like a construction worker even though he owned his own antique business now. He sold old dishes, toys and art online, through his website. "You know what I'm here for," he said, grinning.

I did. Murray turned up at the end of my morning shift almost every day. He always ordered the same thing. I handed him a cup of coffee and two oatmeal "doilies." I called these cookies doilies because as they baked, the dough spread out into crisp circles. They looked like the lace doilies people put under vases to protect their furniture.

"Thanks, Cookie," Murray said as he took the plate. He was the one who gave me the nickname Cookie. Now every regular at the bakery called me that. My real name is Eva.

"You ever going to give me the recipe so I can make these cookies at home?" he asked me.

I shook my head as I smiled shyly at him. We didn't use packaged mixes at this bakery. We baked everything from scratch. I made these cookies from my own recipe.

"Probably better if you don't tell me," he said. "I want a reason to keep coming in here." Murray held my gaze just a little too long, as if he liked me. But I wasn't sure. More to the point, I found it hard to believe he *could* be interested in me. He was such a handsome and accomplished man, with a business of his own.

And me? I just worked here, at this bakery. My hair was tucked in a hairnet because I'd been baking that morning. My apron was covered in flour and butter stains. I never wore makeup to work because it got so hot around the big commercial ovens. I always worked up a sweat. If I did wear mascara, it smudged. What could Murray possibly see in me?

Diana elbowed me as Murray went to his usual table by the window. "Like he needs another reason to come in here," she said. "He's got you."

She grinned at me, but I tried to ignore her. I wiped the counter to hide my embarrassment.

Diana was the owner of the bakery. She was in her sixties now and had owned the bakery-café in this strip mall for more than twenty-five years. The café looked a little dated too. The place could have used some fresh paint and new tables.

But the big windows filled the space with light, and the room always smelled of sweet baked goods. The bakery-café was a favorite hangout, the only place to meet for coffee in this rural area just outside of town.

I had worked at the bakery since my daughter Katie was little. Katie had worked here summers as a teen. Now she took cooking courses at the college in town. But I had never gone to school to learn how to bake. I had learned all that from Diana, on the job. Then I practiced baking at home, making up my own recipes.

"Come on, Eva, when are you going to do something about that?" Diana asked me, nodding at Murray.

"What?" I asked, as if I didn't know.

"He likes you. And I *know* you like him."

I felt my face heat up. Were my feelings for Murray that obvious? "Murray is only being kind," I said.

"You don't give yourself enough credit," Diana said. "Your cookies are truly wonderful, but you're the reason Murray comes in here every morning. I see him watching you when you aren't looking."

He glanced up now to see us watching *him*. Caught, he quickly looked away.

"I don't have time for romance," I said. "I've got a kid, and I've got work. That's more than enough to fill my day."

"Katie is a grown woman now," said Diana. "She's in college. It's time to start thinking about yourself."

"Katie is still living at home. On top of paying for rent and food, I have to pay for her tuition now, the cost of her schooling. After I pay the bills on payday, I have hardly anything left over." I stopped when I saw the look on Diana's face. "I don't mean to complain," I said. "You've been good to me, letting me work overtime when I need the cash."

Diana sighed. "I wish I could give you even more hours, for my sake as well as yours." She rubbed her sore knee. She was about to have an operation on that knee. Standing on her feet for hours each day year after year had taken its toll on her. She looked tired and often winced in pain. "But with the economy the way it is…" She didn't finish her sentence.

I knew things had been hard for her and everyone in the community. When the small department store in this rural strip mall had closed down, one business after another had also closed. But, as Diana often said, people had to eat. There were enough regular customers, like Murray, to keep the bakery going. Even so, I knew Diana had been trying to sell the business so she could retire. The For Sale sign had been up outside the bakery for over a year. Diana had told me she would make sure the new owner kept me on, however. She would make it clear I helped her run the place.

Diana took my hand in hers. "Listen, Eva, since we're on the subject…" She hesitated.

"What is it?"

"I've been meaning to talk to you, not just about your hours, but about your job."

"My job?" I felt my stomach knot.

"As you know, I haven't had any serious offers on the bakery. No one wants to take the place on, not with all these other businesses in the mall shutting down. And I have my knee operation coming up."

She looked around the small bakery-café. The glass counter was full of baked goods. A row of small tables lined the windows. The place smelled of the cinnamon buns baking in the big oven in the kitchen behind us. "I've decided to close the bakery at the end of next month."

I covered my mouth. "Oh no!" I said.

"The tourists will be gone by then," she said. "Labor Day weekend is coming up. Summer is already just about over. I can't keep the place open any longer. I'll have to stay off this knee for several months after the operation."

"I understand," I said. I was sad for Diana—and for our customers. Without this bakery, there would be no place for people in the community to meet. They would have to drive into town just to go out for a cup of coffee. But I was most worried about myself and my daughter. What was I going to do without this job? How was I going to help Katie get through college? She still had another year of schooling in her cooking course.

Diana didn't catch on to my panic right away. "So you'd better do something about

Murray now," she said. "Ask the poor man out. You've been dancing around each other for years. After we close, you won't have an excuse to see him."

I stole a glance at him. He was watching me again, and his face was red. Could he hear our conversation? "Shush," I told Diana. I lowered my voice further. "If he likes me so much, why hasn't he asked *me* out?"

"He's as shy as you are."

"Murray doesn't strike me as shy. He talks up a storm with the other regulars."

"You do too."

"That's part of my job," I said. "And I know everyone here."

"Look, I'm just saying you've both been through a lot when it comes to love."

That much was true. Katie's dad had disappeared from our lives when Katie was a toddler. He didn't even provide child support. The few men I had dated after him didn't want to take on my little family.

In recent years I had given up on the idea of dating altogether.

Murray, on the other hand, had lost his wife to cancer. In the years since, I had never seen him with another woman. I liked that about him. He seemed to be saving himself for someone special. I couldn't believe the someone special might be me.

"Maybe it's time to give Murray that recipe for your doily cookies?" Diana suggested. "Or offer to make some for him at his place?"

"I could never do that." My heart raced at the thought. What if he said no?

"Maybe I should put a bug in his ear." Diana grinned. "Tell him to ask you out."

"You wouldn't do that!" I paused. "Would you?"

"Somebody has to help you two fools get it together."

"I don't have time to think about Murray right now," I said, hoping she'd take the hint. "I've got to focus on finding other work. Katie goes back to college next week. I have enough saved up to cover her tuition, the cost of her course. Other than that, I don't have much money. If I don't find another job right away, I might have to cash in my retirement fund. It's only three or four thousand dollars. That won't last long."

Diana wrapped an arm around me as she finally realized how hard I was taking the news. "I'm so sorry, Eva. I wish I could keep the bakery running. But I'm getting too old. It's taking too much out of me."

"I know," I said. I looked up at her. "But I only know how to bake. I don't have any other skills. What am I going to do?"

Diana didn't have an answer. And I didn't have much time to figure out how I was going to make a living. I had worked in this bakery for nearly fifteen years. Now I would have to start all over again.

I looked around the place and at the customers I knew so well. At the end of the next month I'd be out of a job. I would no longer come here every day. I would visit my old friend Diana, but I might not see Murray again. I wouldn't have my daily excuse to talk to him. I doubted I would ever work up the courage to go visit him. All of a sudden, I felt like my familiar world was crumbling all around me.

Two

I checked the job listings in the local newspapers as soon as I got home. There were no jobs for bakers in town. There were baking jobs in the next big city, but that was too far to drive every day.

I heard the door open, and my daughter skipped in. Everyone said Katie looked a lot like me. Her dark hair was pulled back in a ponytail. Her eyes were brown, and, like me, she didn't wear much makeup. Today she wore jeans and a blue T-shirt with a pun printed on it. It read *I bake because I knead the dough*. Of course, *dough* also means "money."

"Hey, Mom," she said. "How was your day?"

"I've had better," I said.

She took in the worried look on my face. "What's going on? Did something happen?"

"Diana is closing the bakery," I said. "As of the end of September, I'm out of a job."

"Shit." Katie dropped her backpack on the floor and sat on a stool opposite me. "Can I still go to school?"

Trust a kid to think of herself first, I thought. But then, her schooling had also been my first thought.

I put my head in my hands. "To be honest, I don't know. I have to find a job right away, or we'll be living on the streets. I don't have much cash stashed away."

"There must be positions open in other bakeries or in a bakery in a supermarket." Katie pulled her laptop from her backpack and started looking on the Internet. She checked out jobs at the grocery stores and bakeries in the nearby town.

"No openings for bakers, right?" I said.

"Not right now."

"There are bakery jobs in other towns," I said. "But we would have to move."

"I'm just about to go back to college— in town. I'm only halfway through my cooking program. I can't move. Can you get another job here, at another kind of business?"

"All I know is what I learned in Diana's bakery," I said. "I don't know how to do anything else."

"You can go to the college. Take a course. Learn new skills."

"I can't afford that, honey. On top of tuition for your college courses, I still have to pay for rent, food, electricity, our phones."

"Maybe one of us could get a student loan. Or both of us!" Katie thought for a moment. "I saw a poster up at the college. There's an administrative-assistant program starting this week. You could take that course."

"I'm not really sure what an administrative assistant is."

"A receptionist or office clerk. A secretary. You would be the person who keeps the office running and helps everyone else. You'd learn basic office skills, like how to write reports and letters. A friend of mine took the course last year."

"I'm not sure about writing reports and letters. I haven't written much since high school."

"I can help with your writing. I can tutor you."

I put my hand to my mouth. "Oh, that's so embarrassing. My daughter teaching *me*. I should be helping *you* at school."

"You do all the time. You taught me how to cook and bake in the first place, remember? In any case, I'm the reason you didn't finish school."

She was right, in a way. I'd become pregnant with Katie in twelfth grade and had to leave school. Katie's dad wasn't ready to be a father any more than I was ready to be a mother. He had left me not long after Katie was born. I'd had to work to support my daughter and myself from then on. There was no time to finish high school, much less go to college. I did have days when I resented being a single mother. But I didn't want Katie to know that.

"You don't owe me anything," I said. "You've been a gift."

"I know you love me, Mom. But I also know how hard things have been for you. Let me help you out now."

I admired my daughter as she searched the Internet for information on the course. She could do anything she put her mind to. She never seemed afraid to try new things. I had been like her once. Where had that brave part of me gone?

Katie shifted the laptop to show me the college website. "Check it out."

I read over the course information with Katie. The first month was all about working on a computer. I would learn how to manage files and use computer software. There was even a section on using social media and doing research via the Internet. "I don't know much about any of that," I said.

"That's why you take the course— to learn."

"Oh, no!" I said after reading more. "There's an accounting section. I would have to learn business math. I hate math!"

"You use a lot of that kind of math already, Mom. You help Diana with her bookkeeping. Besides, you're taking the course to learn all that. The teacher won't expect you to know everything going in."

"I guess."

"Look," she said, pointing at the laptop screen. "This is great! It says here that when you're done, you'll have all the basic skills you need to work in almost any kind of business office. Classes start later in the morning. You could still work the early-morning shift at the bakery before class."

"At least until Diana closes the bakery." I sat back. Could I really make this happen? Then I shook my head. "Katie, this is all great. But, like you said, I didn't finish high school. I can't go to college, not until I get my high school diploma. And I don't have time to do that now. I have to work."

Katie scrolled down the screen. "It says right here you may not need a high school diploma. If you're a mature student, you can often get into a course because of your work experience. You've helped Diana run her business for years."

That was true. As Diana's knee got worse, I'd started helping more and more. Now I helped her with almost everything. I mixed dough and baked, but I also ordered and picked up supplies. I answered the phone and took orders.

I squinted at the course information on the screen. "But the course starts this week. They won't take me now. It's too late. And I don't even know how to apply."

"They might have space and take last-minute applications. Let's try. We can apply right now." Katie clicked the Apply Online button. "I'll help you fill in the form."

"But how can I afford it? What if I can't get another job with early-morning hours after the bakery closes? Can I go to school if I'm collecting employment insurance?"

Katie checked the government site. "Hmm. Maybe, maybe not. You must prove that you are trying to find a job. If you do find work during class hours, you have to quit going to school."

She clicked back on the college website. "But you may be able to get money for school elsewhere. There are college grants and bursaries for mature people like you who are improving their work skills. Then there are student loans. Tomorrow we'll talk to the education advisor at the college about how to pay for your course. She can help us figure that out."

"Even if I can get funding for the course, that money won't cover all our expenses. I still have to pay rent. And I doubt we'll get enough from grants and student loans."

"I saw a sign in the window of the donut shop in town," Katie said. "They're hiring now that summer is over. The students that worked at that café are going back to school. You could get a job there while you finish the course. With your experience working at the bakery, I know they would hire you."

"I should just take a full-time job there and forget about the course."

"Mom, taking this course will help you get a better job." My daughter took my hand. "I know this all seems scary," she said. "I was nervous when I started college last fall. Everything was so new. I wasn't sure I could handle it all."

"*You* were nervous?" I asked. "You always seem so confident, so sure of yourself."

"You helped me. When things got hard, I always knew I had a safe place to come home to. To you." She patted my hand. "Now it's my turn to help you. I'll drop a class so you can afford to do this. I'll take a job at the donut shop too. We'll piece together enough to get by."

"Oh, Katie. I don't want you to do that."

"A lot of my friends have to work while they go to school, Mom. It's just the way it is. I can make up the dropped course over the summer. Or online." She grinned.

"Come on! Once you get used to school, I know you'll have fun. I'll help out more around the house so you have time to do your homework."

"You already do your share."

"Mom, you've given up so much for me. Let me help you now. Isn't it time you started thinking about yourself?"

I laughed. "Diana said the same thing today."

"Take it as a sign," Katie said.

I started to feel excited. Maybe Diana and my daughter were right. I *could* take this college course and try something new.

"Okay," I said. "Let's apply for that course, before I change my mind."

Katie and I went to work, filling out the application form. When we were done, Katie said, "Let's celebrate!" She eyed the plastic container I had brought home from the bakery, as I did each night. Diana let me take some of the baked goods that hadn't sold. "What did you bring home this time?"

I opened the lid and offered her Murray's favorites, my oatmeal doily cookies.

Three

As soon as I walked into the college classroom my first day, I knew I had overdressed. I'd worn the one dress I owned, bought for Katie's high school graduation. All the other women in the class wore jeans and T-shirts. A few even wore yoga pants.

I sat at the back by the door and pulled out a notepad from my bag. My hands were sweaty, I was so nervous.

I stared at the computer monitor in front of me. There was a computer in front of every student. That made me even more nervous. I did use the computer at the bakery to send brief emails as I ordered supplies. But I wasn't sure how to use the word-processing software.

How would I organize files on this thing? Would I make a fool of myself? I took a deep breath to calm down. As Katie said, I was here to learn all that.

Our teacher introduced herself as Heather, and she wasn't what I'd expected. She was quite a bit younger than me, and pretty. She was dressed smartly but casually. Heather asked students to introduce themselves. When it was my turn, I mumbled my name with my head down. I was used to serving people at Diana's bakery, but I didn't like a crowd looking at me.

Heather told us what textbooks we would have to buy from the college bookstore. She handed out sheets that explained how we would be marked. Then she told us about all the things we would learn in the course.

"In this first month, you'll learn how to use a computer to organize files. We'll also write letters and reports. We'll do other things too, like make ads and pamphlets for promoting a business. How many of you have a laptop at home?"

Everyone in the room raised a hand. I slowly put up mine as well. I didn't own a laptop, but Katie did, of course. I had worked extra hours for Diana so I could buy it for Katie's birthday. She needed it at college.

"And how many of you are on social media?" Heather asked. "Facebook? Twitter?"

Again all the other women put up their hands. I was the only one who didn't. I suddenly felt old, out of it.

"Later we'll learn how to use the Internet to find information," Heather said. "And to promote a business. Okay, let's get started!"

For the rest of the first class, Heather showed us how to log into the online classroom, where we would do a lot of our work.

This Internet site looked confusing at first. I took careful notes in case I forgot something later. At the end of the first class I felt like my head was spinning. Everything was new, and there was so much to take in. I kept telling myself that Katie had felt the same way when she first went to college.

＊

The first week of classes went by quickly. We practiced typing for part of the day. Then we learned computer skills. I worked hard on my assignments and got Katie's help in the evenings. I made sure I handed everything in to my teacher on time. On top of that, I worked the morning shift at Diana's bakery. By the end of the week I was really tired.

As everyone in the class packed up for the day on Friday, my teacher came over to my table. "Eva, can you stay a few minutes?" she asked. "I'd like to talk with you."

"Have I done something wrong?" I asked.

"No, no, nothing like that," she said.

Still, I fretted as I waited for the others to leave. I hadn't received my marks from the week's assignments yet. Maybe I wasn't smart enough to be in this class.

After the last student had left the room, I said, "I'm sorry if my work isn't good enough. I haven't been in a classroom for a long time. I'll try harder."

Heather smiled. "Your work is really good, Eva. I was just a little worried about you. You haven't said anything in class all week. A good part of your mark comes from taking part in class. You'll have to answer questions and work in groups. Learning to communicate, to talk with others, is a big part of every business. In the workplace, you'll have to greet people and answer the phone. You'll also have to exchange information and ideas with the people you work with."

"I do all that at the bakery," I said. I fiddled with the backpack I'd borrowed from my daughter. "I don't know anyone in the class. And like I said, it's been a long time since I've been in school. Being here makes me nervous."

Heather nodded. "Students who sit by the door usually aren't sure if they should be here or not. But Eva, you do belong here. Look." She handed me my week's assignments. I was surprised to see that I'd gotten good marks on most of them.

"I saw on your application that you didn't finish high school," Heather said. "Judging from your work, you must have taken courses over the years."

"No. I've worked at the same bakery for many years. Now Diana is closing it down. She's retiring and couldn't find a buyer."

"Diana is your boss?"

"Yes. She owns the bakery in the strip mall just out of town."

"You're soon out of a job then?"

"That's why I'm taking this course," I said. "I only know how to bake. I need the skills I will learn here to get another job."

"Well, you clearly learned a lot about running a business from working with Diana," Heather said. "Looks like you're going to be one of my star students."

"Really?" I stood a little straighter. "I've been so worried I wouldn't be able to find work. In fact, I wasn't sure I could do the work in this course."

"From what I see in your assignments, you have a natural business sense. Have you ever thought of starting your own business?"

"Oh, I wouldn't know where to begin."

"Most of us know more than we think we do. Tell me what you do at the bakery."

I paused to think. "On the early-morning shift, I start up the big ovens and mix the dough."

"I bet you use math there, don't you?"

"Yes, I guess I do. It's important that everything is measured the same each time. Otherwise the cookies and breads won't taste the same. Once the dough is mixed, I form the cookies or pastries and put them in the oven."

"You use your hands, work fast."

I laughed. She had that right. I worked up a sweat in the kitchen. "There's so much to do," I said. "I have to be really organized. Everything must be planned out ahead of time. The kitchen has to be tidy, with everything in its place."

"See? You already have math and organizational skills. If you can do that, you can organize files on your computer and do some basic accounting."

"I also help Diana with her bookkeeping," I said. My teacher was right. I *did* have more skills than I'd thought.

"And you clearly love what you do," Heather said. "Your face lights up when you talk about working in the kitchen."

"I do love it. I hate the thought of leaving the bakery."

Heather smiled. "So why aren't you running your own small business, selling your own baked goods?"

I stopped to think for a moment. Maybe I *could* run Diana's bakery. There was just one big thing I lacked. "I don't have enough money," I said.

She jotted down the name of a website on a piece of paper and gave it to me. "Check out this organization on the Internet. They offer loans and advice to small businesses. They may be able to help. You will need a business plan before you ask them for a loan. They'll want to see it. In any case, creating that plan is the first step to starting any business."

I took the website address she offered me. "I don't really know what a business plan is."

"You're a baker, so think of a business plan as a recipe for making your business. You list the things you need first. Then you write down how to mix those ingredients together to make it happen."

"I make a list of the equipment I need. And the supplies."

"Yes, and where will you make your baked goods? Who will you sell them to? How much will the equipment and rent cost? How much money do you already have? Where will you get the rest of the money you need? A good business plan may convince an investor to lend you the money to start your business."

She pointed at the Internet address she had just given me. "You'll find a sample business plan on this website. You can use that to make your own plan."

"My own recipe for baking up a business, you mean," I said, grinning. When I said it like that, making a business plan didn't seem so hard. I created and tested new recipes all the time. But after thinking about it a moment, I said, "I just can't see myself running my own business. There's so much to think about."

"Well, when you're finished this course, you certainly won't have any trouble finding a job working for someone else," Heather said. She smiled. "Though you could use some help with your writing." She tapped my assignments. She had circled spelling mistakes and made corrections on many of them.

"My daughter said she would help me with that," I said. "She's going to college here as well."

"It's good to have someone to study with at home. But I'm here to help too. I can always stay after class to work with you."

"You would do that?"

"As I said, you are one of my star students."

I felt giddy as I picked up my backpack to leave.

Heather called to me before I went out the door. "And Eva, if you change your mind about starting up a small business, let me know. Maybe I can help."

I smiled in response, but the idea of owning a business seemed out of my reach. Still, I pocketed the website address my teacher had given me.

Four

The next morning I felt happy. I hummed as I whipped together the day's batch of doily cookies and served customers. When I caught Murray watching me from his table, I actually smiled at him. All of a sudden I didn't feel so shy around him anymore. My teacher's encouragement had given me new confidence.

"What's got into you?" Diana asked. She glanced at Murray, who was still grinning at me. "Did you take my advice and finally have that date with Murray?"

"No!" I slapped Diana playfully on the arm. "Stop teasing me about Murray."

"Why are you so chipper then?"

"My teacher says I'm her star student."

"Of course you are! I don't know why you feel you need to take that course. You do everything I do around here. You could be running this bakery yourself."

"Oh, but I'm learning so much," I said. "I'm already typing much faster, and I'm a lot more comfortable using the computer now. Last night Katie helped me set up a Facebook account. We should have made a Facebook page for the bakery. You could have used social media to bring in more customers." I paused. "But I guess now that you're closing, it's too late for that."

One of our regular customers, Lucy, came up to the counter. She handed me a twenty to pay for the tea and shortbread cookies I had brought her earlier. She was in her eighties, frail and bent over. She needed a cane, and yet she made a point of walking her dog from her house to the bakery twice a day, morning and afternoon.

"Leaving already?" I asked her.

"I was late getting out this morning. If I don't hurry back, I'll miss my show."

I handed her the change.

"Did I hear right that you're closing shop?" she asked Diana. She must have overheard our conversation.

"Have to," Diana said. "My knee operation is next month. I can't bake if I can't stand all day."

Lucy turned to me, looking worried. "Can't you take over?"

"I only work here, Lucy," I said. "I don't have the money to buy the bakery."

"Can't you manage it while Diana's away?"

"Eva couldn't run the place by herself," said Diana. "And I can't afford to pay someone else to help her, not over the winter. Besides, it's time for me to retire. I can't keep the bakery open any longer."

"Well, what am I going to do?" Lucy asked. "This is the only company I've got, other than my dog." She looked around at the regulars. Many nodded in agreement.

"I'm sure your kids will visit you," Diana said, trying to lighten Lucy's mood.

"They live too far away," Lucy said. "I'll be stuck in that house all alone."

I put a hand on her arm. "You won't be alone," I said. "I'll make a point of visiting. I'll bring Katie. You remember my daughter."

"You'd do that? Bring me some of your shortbread too?"

I laughed. "Of course."

"Maybe it won't be so bad then," she said.

I patted her hand before she turned to leave.

"It's funny Lucy asked me if I would run the bakery," I said to my boss. "My teacher said I should think about running my own business."

"I wish you could take over the bakery." Diana waved at Lucy as she left. I waved at her too as Murray opened the door for her. We all watched as the old woman walked her dog back down the road. Murray joined us at the counter, holding his hat. I found myself disappointed to realize he was about to leave too.

"Losing this place will be hard on all of us," he said, nodding at the other regulars. "Not just the retired folks. I work at home alone, so coming here is an important part of my day."

"Well, maybe Eva will bring cookies over to your house too," Diana said.

"Diana!" I cried, warning her that she had crossed a line.

But Diana only nudged me, coaxing me to say something to Murray.

"I'd like that," Murray said to me.

He held my gaze, waiting for a response, but I just couldn't get the words out. Was he only being nice because Diana had put him on the spot?

Finally, he said, "Well, I'd better get going myself. I've got several pieces to ship off today." He looked hurt as he turned and left the bakery.

I faced Diana. "Why did you invite me over to his place?" I glanced at the customers who were turned our way, listening in. "You embarrassed us both."

"That man is wasted on you," she said. "He practically asked you out, and you ignored him."

I saw two of the regulars, both old men, shaking their heads at my foolishness.

I lowered my voice so only Diana could hear. "I just didn't know what to say."

"You could have told Murray you would love to bring him cookies. You could have said you'd like to spend a little time with him. Don't you like him?"

"Of course I do."

"Then what's the problem?"

"I don't know," I said miserably. "I guess I'm afraid to risk it."

"With Murray?"

I threw up my hands. "With anything, it seems. Katie practically had to push me to take that course. I never would have done it on my own. After my teacher called me her star student, I started to feel sure of myself again. But then, just now, I couldn't work up the nerve to talk with Murray."

I turned my back to the customers to hide my emotions. I thought I might cry. "What happened to me?" I asked Diana. "I used to think big, like Katie. I used to believe in myself, that I could do whatever I wanted. Then I stopped believing I could do anything more than work and pay the bills. Now I'm not even sure I can do that."

Diana sat on a stool and rubbed her knee. "I think we just get tired," she said. "We have kids. We put them first. We work.

We get home and do chores. At the end of the day we're worn out. We don't have energy for dreaming big or even for taking care of ourselves."

I looked again at Lucy walking slowly down the road with her dog. "And the years go by so fast."

"Yes, they do."

I turned back to Diana. "I don't want to spend another decade just getting through my day," I said. "I feel—" I stopped, unsure how to put it into words.

"I understand," Diana said. "Your daughter is grown up, and she's about to head out on her own. Katie is going to leave a big gap in your life when she does."

"Yes, that's it exactly."

"I know all about it. I opened this place around the time my own kids went off on their own." Diana watched me for a moment.

"What?" I asked her. "I know that look. You've got one of your ideas."

"Why *don't* you take over the bakery?"

I went back to the work area and started putting together my next batch of dough. "I thought about it as soon as you put the business up for sale. But I don't have the money to buy it. And even if I did, like you said, I couldn't run this place."

"I said you couldn't run this place *alone*. You know how to do everything. And you have Katie. At the end of this year she'll complete her training. She'll be a certified cook and baker. You and Katie get along so well. She's already worked here summers."

I thought about it for a moment. What Diana said was true. Katie and I were very close. I was the only family she had. We did work well together. And she would certainly have the skills to run the bakery alongside me. But I just didn't have the means. "It's a lovely dream. But like I said, I don't have the money to buy the business from you."

Diana sighed. "I would love to hand the bakery over to you, free of charge. But I'm not sure I have enough to retire on as it is. When this knee heals, I may end up working at some fast-food joint. I couldn't sell the business. I hope I can at least sell the equipment in here."

I scanned the mixing machines and ovens, all the baking equipment I wish I owned myself. Everything I needed to run my own bakery was here, waiting for me. If only I could come up with the money.

"My teacher said if I wanted to start a business, I needed a business plan. She said I might be able to use that plan to get a loan."

"That was my first step in starting up this place," Diana said. "I worked out a business plan, then took it to the bank."

"I really don't know where to start."

"If I can make a business plan, you sure as hell can."

I put the cookie dough under the mixer and started it up. "I'm going to check out sample business plans on the Internet tonight," I said. "Maybe making one isn't as hard as I thought."

"That's the spirit," Diana said.

"Katie can help me."

"And so can I. Give me a call when you need numbers. I can tell you exactly what it costs to run this place each month. With Katie and me helping you, you'll have that business plan written up in no time."

"It's a plan!" I said.

Diana grinned at my bad joke. We both went back to work with a bit more energy in our steps.

Five

When I got home that evening, Katie had supper waiting for me. When I thanked her, she said, "I figured you'd be tired. You're been up since four."

I *was* tired. My shift at the bakery started at five in the morning. When my shift ended, I went straight to class. "I had an interesting conversation with Diana this morning," I said.

"Oh?" Katie set my plate in front of me. Since she'd started her cooking class, even her simple meals were served elegantly. Tonight she had made pan-seared salmon with asparagus.

"She encouraged me to take over the bakery," I said. "I'm thinking about it."

"Well, it's about time," Katie said. "I've been telling you to do that since Diana put the bakery up for sale."

"I know. I just didn't think I could until now."

"Taking that course has been good for you, hasn't it?"

I nodded. "I'm starting to see I *can* make things happen for myself. I just need a clear goal and a plan." I paused to taste the salmon. "How would you feel about working in the bakery again? Or even running it with me?"

"You mean go into business with you? I would love that!"

"Really?"

"Of course, Mom. We're a team. We always have been."

"You've got that right."

"What's the first step?"

"Both Diana and my teacher told me I need a business plan." I fished out the scrap of paper Heather had given me with the website address on it. "Heather told me about a site I can go to for information on how to start a small business. They even offer loans. But I need to write up a business plan first."

Katie pushed back her plate. "Well, let's get started!"

"Now?"

"No time like the present." She pulled her laptop out of her bag and set it on the table in front of us.

"May I?" I asked, pointing to her computer.

"Of course!" Katie grinned. She thought my sudden interest in computers was funny. I had finally caught up with the times.

I typed in the website address my teacher had given me. I looked around until I found a sample business plan. Then I saved the file on the laptop. With Katie's help, I started filling it out.

All the things I needed to think about were laid out in the form. I just filled in the boxes step by step. There *was* a lot to think about though. And I didn't have all the answers. I had to do more research on the Internet and phone Diana. At least I had my boss to help me out.

The first thing I had to do on the form was describe what kind of business I wanted to run. That was the easy part. I wanted to run Diana's bakery. And I knew who my customers were. I also knew there was no competition in the area. Diana's place was the only bakery-café in the community.

I outlined my own skills, why I thought I could run this business. Now that I had gained some confidence, I found this easy too. I had helped Diana run her bakery for years.

The bakery would be located right where it was. And I knew what equipment

I needed. The ovens, mixers and pots and pans were already there too. I even knew where to order my supplies. Diana had given me the company names and numbers I would call to order my flour, sugar and other ingredients. I would buy containers for my baked goods from another place. If I wanted, I could order everything online. I typed all that into the business-plan form.

There were other questions on the form, like who would work at my bakery? That would only be Katie and me to start. Diana said she might help once her knee healed up.

"But what are you going to call your bakery?" Katie asked.

"Cookies, of course," I said.

Katie grinned. "Of course."

I was less certain how I would promote my business. Diana put ads in the newspaper. But I knew now that I could do a lot of my advertising online through social media.

I was even less sure how to answer the biggest question. How was I going to afford to buy the bakery? I would have to get a loan. The organization on this website offered loans to small-business owners. But I also knew I had to come up with some of my own money. I just wasn't sure how much. I would have to cash in my retirement fund. But there wasn't much money there.

Even with Diana's and Katie's help, it took me several days to finish my business plan. Diana told me it had taken her much longer than that to do her plan. She'd had to phone all over to get the information she needed. I was grateful for her help.

✳

When I felt I'd finished my business plan, I showed it to my teacher at the end of a class. Heather was delighted. "You created a business plan? Congratulations! I'm so excited to hear you want to start your own business."

"It's not exactly a new business," I said. "I want to take over Diana's bakery."

"Oh?" The excitement on Heather's face faded as she read through my plan.

"Did I do something wrong?" I asked. "I used the sample business plan from the website address you gave me."

"Not at all. This is a fine plan. You've done a lot of work, and you can use this in the future."

"In the future?" I asked. "Why not now?"

"When I suggested you start your own business, I was thinking of a home-based bakery." Heather handed my business plan back to me. "I think your goal of taking over Diana's bakery may be too ambitious," she said.

"Ambitious?"

"You may be trying to do too much too soon," Heather said. "You don't have enough of a down payment to buy the bakery business or even the equipment.

Can you bake at home instead? Maybe you can sell your baked goods at a farmers' market."

"But I want to keep Diana's bakery open. I want to run a bakery-café."

"I'm sure you could run your own bakery in time. But right now I don't think you have enough money to take it over. Even if you apply for a loan, you'll need some of your own money. The lender will also ask if you own something of value to secure the loan. If your business fails, the lender needs to know they can get their money back. Do you own your own home? Or property?"

"No, I rent."

"I think you may be out of luck then."

"But I have an appointment with a loan officer in the morning."

"I'll look forward to hearing how that goes," said Heather. "I'm sure your loan officer will give you some good advice.

But don't be discouraged if you don't get the money. I think you will have to start smaller. Work up to that dream of running a bakery. Over time."

I felt discouraged already. I must have looked upset too, because Heather put a hand on my shoulder. "There are always setbacks," she said. "Don't let them stop you from making your dream happen."

I felt angry with Heather as I packed my bag to leave. She didn't think I could get that loan. Well, I thought, I would show her. Then I caught myself. Where had that confidence come from? I realized in that moment just how much I wanted to own my own bakery.

Six

I stumbled in to my afternoon shift at the bakery, feeling miserable. I'd had to miss my usual morning shift to attend the appointment with the loan officer. That meant I also had to miss my afternoon class so I could work this shift. With the bakery about to close, I couldn't afford to miss even one day of work.

When I arrived, Murray was sitting at his table. He nodded at me as I headed to the counter. "What's Murray doing here?" I asked Diana as I tied on my apron. "I thought he only came to the bakery mornings."

"He only comes when *you're* here," she said. "He's been waiting for you. That's his third cup of coffee." She lowered her voice. "How did the appointment with the loan officer go?"

Before I could answer, the bell over the door tinkled as someone came in. It was old Lucy. "We'll talk about that later," I told Diana.

"Beautiful day," Lucy said as I brought her tea and shortbread.

I looked out the window. The fall colors only served to remind me that the bakery was about to close. "I guess," I said.

"Why are you so sour today?" Lucy asked. "I'm the cranky one, remember?"

I forced a smile, but Lucy knew something was up. "What's happened?" she asked.

"It's nothing."

As I turned back to the counter, Murray waved me over. "You want a refill?" I asked him.

"No, thank you. I've had more than enough coffee today." He stood up too quickly, nearly knocking his cup off the table. When he steadied it, I noticed his hands were shaking. "I was hoping to talk to you though. I was wondering—" He cleared his throat. "Would you like to have dinner with me sometime? Maybe this weekend?"

The café suddenly went quiet. I looked around. Not only Diana, but Lucy and several of the regulars had turned to watch us. It seemed Murray and I had been of interest to everyone more than I knew.

I stood there for a moment uncertain what to do. Murray had caught me off guard, and now all these people were watching. "I'm sorry, Murray," I said finally. "I just don't have time. I'm working morning shifts. I'm in class during the day. Then I have homework evenings and weekends—" When I saw the look on his face, I stopped. I had hurt his feelings.

"I understand," he said. He glanced around at the other regulars and put on his hat. "I've got to get back to work." He fled from the bakery.

I had embarrassed him in front of everyone. I knew I might never see him again. The café would close in a few days. He was unlikely to come back now.

I went back to the counter with my head down. The conversation in the bakery picked up again. I saw old Lucy push herself up from the table and toddle toward the counter with her cane. "What the hell did you go and do that for?" she asked me.

"I'm not sure what you mean."

"Why did you say no to that man?"

Diana put a hand on my arm. "You know how long Murray's been working up the nerve to ask you out."

"You put him up to it," I said. I suddenly felt angry at Diana. "You told him to ask me out."

Diana put her hands on her hips. "I did no such thing. He did that all on his own."

"You didn't talk to him about me, how I feel about him?"

"No, I didn't. I didn't have to."

I crossed my arms as I watched Murray drive away. I felt so foolish now. "It doesn't matter," I said. "It's just not meant to be. I really don't have time for dating right now."

"That's baloney," said Lucy. She waved a cane at the regulars at their tables. "We can all see how much you like him. You light up when he comes in every morning."

Several of the old men nodded.

"What's going on with you today anyway?" asked Lucy. "I've never seen you snap at Diana like that."

I sighed. "I got some bad news this morning. I wanted to keep the bakery open.

I tried to get a loan today, but my teacher was right. The loan officer said she wouldn't lend me the money to buy the bakery."

"I was turned down for a loan too," Diana said. "I had to go back to work and save up. Then I tried again, and I got my loan. It took me a couple of years before I could afford to open this place."

"But you're about to close the bakery," I said. "I don't have a couple of years."

"There must be another way to get that money," said Lucy. "Can you take a mortgage out on your house? Use the value of your home to get the loan?"

"That's the problem. I rent. I've never made enough to own my own home."

Diana put her hand on my arm. "I'm so sorry, Eva. I wish I could have afforded to pay you more all these years. You're not just an employee. You're my friend."

"So you're just giving up?" Lucy asked me. "I never pegged you as a quitter."

"What else *can* I do?"

"Why not ask lover boy? Murray's made a pile of money off his business. Why not ask him for a loan? I'm sure he'd love to help you out."

"I don't want to owe him money." I paused. *"Especially* if we ever do start to date."

"You're a wise woman, Eva," Diana said. "I wouldn't want to put myself in that position either. Not a good way to start a relationship."

"How about you then?" Lucy asked Diana. "Can you give her a loan?"

"I wouldn't want to owe a friend either," I said.

"Don't think of it like that," said Lucy. "Diana would invest in your business. You would make money here in the bakery. Diana would get her share, based on how much money she put into the business."

Diana shook her head. "Like I told Eva, I barely have enough to retire. I may even be looking for work myself down the road."

"I'd invest in your business if I had any money," said Lucy.

I smiled sadly. "Thanks, Lucy. That's kind of you to say."

"I'm serious," she said. "I've been coming to this bakery for years. And I've been watching you, Eva. You're a smart cookie." She laughed at her own pun. She knew Murray and almost all the regulars called me Cookie. "You could run this place as well as Diana. Better."

"Hey!" Diana said, grinning.

"No offense," said Lucy. "I just think this bakery could use a new owner. Someone to put energy into it, freshen up the place. I know Eva would do that."

"You're right, Lucy," Diana said. "She would."

"A community needs a business like this one," said Lucy. "Attract enough customers with this bakery, and other business owners would want to open their stores here too. Close the bakery down, and the last of the businesses here are likely to close too. We'd lose the heart of our village. People will start to move away."

I hadn't thought of it like that. I knew our customers wouldn't have a place to meet once the bakery closed. But I hadn't thought about how much the community would lose once this bakery was gone. Keeping it alive suddenly wasn't just a personal dream. I needed to find a way to reopen the bakery here, not just for Katie and me, but for this community.

Seven

At supper that night I took the problem to my daughter. "I'm so sorry I can't buy the bakery right now," I said. "I saw how excited you were about the idea." I took her hand. "But I'm not giving up. I'm going to open my own bakery-café right where Diana's bakery is now. I don't care how long it takes. I just don't know *how* I'm going to do it."

"Do what you always do," Katie said. "Bake from scratch."

"I'm not following."

"Diana's bakery is like a packaged cake mix. All the hard work is done for you. If you had the money, you wouldn't have to do much to reopen the bakery."

"But I don't have the money."

"So you start from scratch. All you really need is a kitchen. And a few supplies. You don't need a storefront. Just sell your baked goods at the farmers' market."

"I won't make enough money if I only sell at the market, especially if I want to open a bakery." I looked around the room. "This kitchen is too small, in any case. The government also has rules about selling food made in a home kitchen. They'll only let you do that if you sell at a farmers' market. I need a big commercial kitchen if I'm going to sell anywhere else."

"Then you find a kitchen you can rent."

I thought for a moment. "There's that pizza joint on the highway. They only open afternoons and evenings. Maybe I could rent their commercial kitchen mornings. Or there's that Greek restaurant on the way into town. Churches often have commercial kitchens for rent. So do recreation centers and even golf clubs."

"I've got a better idea," said Katie. "The community hall is just up the road. It has a big commercial kitchen. It would be free during the week. Probably most weekends too. There aren't many events there anymore."

"You're right," I said. "And renting the hall kitchen would likely cost much less than the other places." I grabbed a notepad and scribbled *Hall*.

"We could sell at that indoor farmers' market in town. It runs most of the year."

"The pie shop in town also sells pies in grocery stores," I said. "I could take samples of our cookies to supermarkets and restaurants and see if they would sell them."

"Yes!" Katie leaned forward, excited. "You remember that fundraiser the school put on? We sold frozen cookie dough. The school made a ton of money with that one.

People like to bake their own cookies, but they don't have time to make the dough. Why not sell cookie dough? Then all people have to do is bake the stuff."

"I really like that idea." I thought for a moment. "I would need different containers, small buckets for the dough."

"No problem," said Katie. "I can order them online."

"And we would need a freezer. But there is a big freezer at the community hall." I wrote down our ideas. This would be the start of my new business plan. I glanced up at Katie. "This might work," I said.

"So what are you going to call *this* business?"

"Isn't that obvious?" I said. "Cookie's Dough."

"Hah!" Katie laughed. "I like it. I hope you make lots of dough with Cookie's Dough."

"I hope so too. I'll need a pile of cash to reopen the bakery-café." I tapped my pencil on the pad of paper. "So how are we going to get the word out? We'll need to promote the business. Can you set up a Facebook page for Cookie's Dough?"

"Of course! But my own teacher says the best way to promote a restaurant is by word of mouth. She told us to focus on the quality of the food. If your food is really good, people will tell other people about your business. And Mom, your cookies are great. We just have to offer people samples, and the cookies will sell themselves. Let's start with the college. You can offer students a cookie. Once they taste one, I know they'll want to buy the cookie dough."

I scribbled all that down. "Okay. I think we have a plan. My first step is to rent the hall kitchen. I'll only be able to make cookies during evenings in the first few months. I'm finishing my course and working mornings at that donut shop starting next week. But maybe once the cookies really start to sell, I can afford to make cookies full-time. I know the rental rates at the community hall are reasonable."

"Murray is in charge of hall rentals, isn't he?"

"Oh no! You're right! I don't think I can face Murray. He asked me out today."

"Murray asked you out? That's awesome, Mom!"

"I said no. I embarrassed him in front of everyone."

"Oh, Mom, *why*? He's such a nice guy."

"I know. It wasn't him. Or...it was in a way. He's handsome. He's successful. He has his own business and a really great house. What's he going to think of me? I rent. In a week, I'll have to work in a donut shop to pay the bills."

"Murray likes *you*, Mom. He doesn't care what you do for a job."

"But what if he gets to know me better and doesn't like me after all?"

Katie paused to think for a moment. "You've liked Murray for a long time."

I nodded. I'd had a crush on Murray for years.

"You've hung on to that dream of him, that fantasy of him, for a long time. Maybe you're afraid of losing that dream? Afraid of getting hurt?"

I looked up at my daughter. "How'd you get to be so smart?" I asked.

"I take after my mother." Then she thought some more. "It's the same with running your own bakery, isn't it? You've dreamed of that for a long time. But you're afraid that if you fail—"

I finished her sentence. "I won't have that to dream about anymore either. You're right, Katie. I'm afraid to try. I'm afraid to fail."

"But if you don't try, you'll never make that dream happen. You won't have your own business." She paused. "Or Murray."

"But I *am* scared. What if my cookie business doesn't work out? What if I make cookie dough and no one buys it?"

"So we eat a lot of cookies," said Katie. "Or we give them away."

"But I can't afford to lose the money I would spend on all those baking supplies. And you would have dropped your course for nothing."

"Mom, who doesn't like cookies? You aren't going to lose money. You'll make lots of dough. Get it?"

"Yeah yeah, I got the joke the first time," I said. My daughter and her awful puns. But she was right. I had to try, or I wouldn't make my dream happen. I wanted to run my own bakery business, even if that meant starting out small at first. I also wanted to get to know Murray better. I just hoped I hadn't already messed that up.

"And listen, Mom, I'm in. I want to run this business with you, even if it's just a home-based business at first."

"Really?"

"I'm going to drop another course so I have the time to bake."

"No, Katie. You can't drop any more classes."

"Don't worry, Mom. I'll make up the courses later. I may even be able to earn credit from working with you. My cooking course is a co-op program. We get credit for working at cafés and bakeries. That means my work counts as a course toward finishing the program. Either way, right now we've got to get this business going. We can use the money from my dropped courses to buy supplies. You won't need much to get things going if you rent the commercial kitchen at the hall."

"You really think we can make a go of it?"

"Yes! And it won't be long before you can open your bakery-café."

"All right," I said. "Let's do this." Then I laughed at myself. "You know what I'm most frightened of at the moment?"

"Stepping out on your own?"

I shook my head. "Facing Murray."

Eight

I stood at Murray's front door, trying to work up the courage to knock. His truck was in the yard, so I knew he was home. I had botched things so badly when he asked me out that I really didn't want to face him. He wouldn't want to see me either. I was certain of it. He hadn't returned to the bakery, even on closing day. What was I doing here? I turned to walk away, clutching the small bucket I had brought for him.

But then Murray opened the door. "Eva!" he called after me. "I heard you drive up. Did you want something?"

"No, I—" I stared at the small white bucket in my hands, embarrassed that he had caught me slinking away. Finally I just held out my gift. "I brought you something."

He took the bucket from me. "What's this?"

"Cookie dough," I said. "For my oatmeal doily cookies. Enough for a couple of batches. You can store it in your freezer. I figured you'd want a supply now that the bakery has closed."

"That was kind of you," he said, but he didn't invite me in. "I'm sorry to see the bakery go. It was my second home."

"I wish your last visit there had been... happier," I said.

"Yes, well..." He fiddled with the handle on the bucket as we stood in silence. Then he pointed a thumb back inside the house. "I should get back to work. Thanks for this." He started to close the door.

But I had come this far. I took a step forward. "I understand you're the person to talk to about renting the hall."

Murray turned back to me, still holding the door. "Ah, I see. That's why you're here." He looked a little annoyed, but nodded. "Yes, I handle the hall rentals."

"I'd like a long-term rental. I imagine I'll have to sign a contract." I paused. "May I come in?"

"Yes. Yes, of course."

I followed him into his kitchen. The house was small but bright. Even though he ran his antique business from his house, he kept things tidy. I saw a long work table in the next room, covered in neat piles of boxes. There he packaged the antiques that he shipped to customers by courier. He sold everything online, through his website.

"I suppose I should offer you coffee and some of these cookies," he said.

"That only seems fair. I served *you* all those years." I grinned to make it clear I was joking, but he still didn't smile.

I sat on a stool at the counter as he poured us each a cup of coffee. Then he turned on the oven and opened the bucket of cookie dough. "I do love these cookies," he said as he spooned the dough onto a cookie sheet. "I'll buy more dough, if you're selling."

"Actually, that's why I want to rent the community hall. I'm going into business for myself, making cookie dough for sale. I understand the hall has a licensed commercial kitchen."

Murray sat with me as he waited for the oven to heat. "Yes, the kitchen is government inspected and certified. One woman ran evening cooking classes there last year. Another operated a catering business from the hall until she could afford to lease a place of her own."

"I want to start up my cookie-dough business there." I patted the bucket of cookie dough. "I'll sell frozen cookie dough as well as baked cookies."

"It's a good idea. You can sign the rental agreement today." He paused. "You may still need a permit to cook at the hall. And do you have a business license?"

I felt my shoulders sag. "Yet another thing to think about!" I said.

"No matter what kind of business you start, you have to look into government licenses and permits."

"I know, I know." I had seen Diana's business license and the health inspector's permit on the bakery wall.

"There are other things you'll have to check into as well. I had to register the name of my business through a government website. I also arranged for business insurance with a local broker."

"Starting a business is just so complicated!" I said, throwing up my hands.

"Life is complicated," he said, and he gave me a wounded look. I realized then just how much I had hurt him. And for no good reason. I really liked Murray. I had rejected him only because I didn't believe in myself.

Another uncomfortable silence stretched out between us. Finally I broke the ice. "Listen, I want to apologize for how I treated you the other day. I embarrassed you in front of everyone at the bakery."

"What do you expect me to say?" Murray asked.

"I know I hurt you."

"I get it. You're not interested in me. You don't have to bring it up again."

I took a deep breath to brace myself. "The truth is, I would love to have supper with you. The other day, I was just feeling—"

"Scared?"

I nodded, laughing a little. "Terrified, actually."

He finally smiled, and I felt relieved. "Me too!" he said. "I've wanted to ask you out for a long time. But I could never work up the nerve. When Diana said she was closing the bakery, I figured I'd better ask before I lost my chance."

"I'm so sorry. You caught me off guard, asking me in front of everyone like that."

Murray nodded. "I should have waited until closing time, after they left."

"There was a bigger problem," I admitted. "I just couldn't figure out why you'd be interested in me. I thought once you really got to know me—"

"Oh, Eva, you're a bright spot in my life, just as you were for all the people who came into Diana's bakery. Don't you know that?"

"I was only doing my job."

"You did so much more. There's a lot of lonely people in the community.

Old people without family, like Lucy. People like me, who have lost someone they loved. You always made time to chat. I can't tell you what a difference your kindness made in my life. It got me through a hard time after my wife died."

I grew shy again.

Murray sat back. "I've said too much."

"No, it's fine. I'm flattered. I just didn't think I was doing anything special."

"That's what makes you wonderful." He took my hand. "And Eva, after all these years, I *do* know you. And I'm *very* interested." He paused as he took in my expression. "Now I *have* said too much."

I smiled, but he was right. His attention *did* made me shy. I changed the subject. "Do you think I could start using the hall this weekend? I'd like to work on my recipes for frozen cookie dough."

"No one else is renting it. You can start first thing in the morning, if you like. I have the spare key here." He pulled the key from a small rack by the door and gave it to me. "Tell me more about this business of yours. How will you sell your cookie dough?"

"I can't afford a storefront like Diana's—at least, not right away. I'm hoping to sell cookies and dough by word of mouth. I'll offer samples at the farmers' market and the college to start. Maybe I can get my frozen dough into a few grocery stores and cafés in town. Eventually, I hope to get orders from other businesses, say, for conferences and events."

"Like the children's festival they hold in town in the summer."

"Yes."

"Have you thought about running an online bakery?"

"I'm not sure what that is."

"You know I run an online antique business. Same thing. You sell your cookie dough from a website on the Internet.

You might sell just one or two tubs of cookie dough to people like me or Lucy. Or you might sell in bulk to businesses buying cookies for employees."

"Or, like I said, for events like business conferences."

"Exactly. I use couriers to ship my stock. I imagine you would deliver your cookies and dough to your customers yourself."

"That's my plan."

"No matter how you sell your baked goods, you'll need a website. A website is an online storefront. People can see what you sell and place orders on the site."

"I have no idea how to make a website."

"But I do. I made my own. There are many online companies now that make it easy. I could probably pull a website together for you this weekend."

"I couldn't afford to pay you."

The oven beeped as it reached the right temperature. Murray slid the cookie sheet into the oven. "Pay me in cookie dough," he said as he closed the door. "Say, a three-month supply."

"That isn't enough."

"It's more than enough. And it would give me an excuse to see you again."

I tucked a strand of hair behind my ear. "Maybe you don't need an excuse," I said. Then I looked down, shocked at my own boldness. I wouldn't have been brave enough to say that before.

"Maybe I don't." Murray took my hand again. "And maybe we don't have to be scared of each other anymore." He grinned.

I looked down at his big hand holding mine. "You know, I can't imagine you being scared of anything," I said. "Especially me. You're so capable. You built this beautiful home and your own business."

"It has been a very long time since I asked a woman out. I wasn't sure you would say yes. Taking a risk is always hard."

He looked around at the house, at the antiques scattered on a second work table in the next room. "The same was true of my business. I wasn't sure at first if I could make a go of it. It took a long time for me to work up the courage to leave my job and start my own business."

I squeezed his hand, then let go and sat back, thinking of all the work ahead of me. "There are so many things to do, so many steps to go through," I said. "Now I have to visit government offices for licenses and permits. And I have to buy insurance and register my business name too. I hadn't thought of that until you told me."

"There *is* a lot to think about," said Murray. "But you can tackle it by making a list and checking things off one by one. For the business license, you go to the town office and fill in a form. You talk to the local health inspector for the permit. I can help you with that, if you like."

"It would be so much easier to give up my dream of owning a bakery and work for someone else."

"I know exactly what you're going through," Murray said. "I knew a lot about antiques. I collected them for years. But what did I know about running an online business? I made mistakes along the way. But I took a chance and walked through the steps it took to reach my goal. In the end, I made this business work."

"I just hope I can do the same," I said.

Murray stood and kissed me on the cheek. "I know you can," he said. He opened the oven, and the sweet smell of my baking cookies filled the room. In that moment, I believed he was right.

Nine

*K*atie and I carried several buckets of cookie dough into my classroom to show the students. I also brought samples of each kind of cookie dough I hoped to sell, baked into fresh cookies.

"What's all this?" my teacher asked, smiling. The other students crowded around to try the cookies.

"Katie and I started a business," I said.

"Cookie's Dough," Katie announced.

"What do you think?" I asked my classmates.

They all grinned and gave me the thumbs-up as they ate the cookies. Several students took seconds.

"My kids will love these," one of the students said. "I never have time to mix up cookie dough myself. I'll take a bucket."

"Me too," said another.

Soon I had sold all the buckets of dough I had brought. Katie collected the cash and wrote down the amount. I knew from working for Diana, and from my class, how important it was to keep good records. I needed to know how much I was making and how much I was spending on supplies. I would need to account for everything when I did my taxes.

"I'll buy some as well," said my teacher.

"I hope you don't mind my bringing the cookie dough in," I said. "I wanted to see what people thought of it and if it would sell. Katie thought the college was a good place to start."

"I think it's a great idea." She finished her cookie. "How are you going to market the cookie dough?"

"I have a website. Murray calls it my online storefront."

"Murray?" my teacher asked.

"He made the website for me," I said.

"Murray is Mom's boyfriend," Katie said.

I smiled shyly at that. Dating Murray was all so new and thrilling. "We're hoping to sell through word of mouth," I said. "We're handing out samples at the farmers' market. We'll also try restaurants and grocery stores around town. I'm hoping if people get a taste of these cookies, they'll want to buy more."

Heather took another bite of her cookie. "Then let's help you get the word out," she said. "Class," she called out. "Eva has given us the perfect opportunity to learn about advertising. We're going to come up with a marketing plan for her business, Cookie's Dough. Let's help her promote her cookies."

To start, Heather asked me to show the class my website. Murray had done a terrific job. There were pictures of me and Katie baking and close-up photos of cookies. The website had a description of the cookie dough we sold. It also had my email address and cell-phone number on it so customers could place orders any time.

Then I showed the class the social-media accounts Katie had set up for our business. Katie had posted photos of cookies and information on how to buy our cookies.

"Let's help Eva by liking or following her business on her social-media sites. Tell others how good her cookies are! Who's willing to offer a review of her cookies?"

Everyone was, as it turned out. They all loved my cookies. The other students in my class recommended my cookies and dough to their friends on their social-media sites. Katie had been right to urge me to bring samples into class. The cookies sold themselves. I was sure now that if I took samples of my dough and cookies into local stores and restaurants, I could sell them there as well.

Ten

A year later, I found myself back at the old bakery location in the strip mall. But this time, the bakery was mine. The walls were freshly painted and covered with big, colorful photos of cookies. Outside, a sign over the door read *Cookie's Bakery*. And beside that, a banner announced *Grand Opening!*

Inside, Katie and Diana served customers at the counter. Diana worked for me now that her knee was healed. Retired, she found she could use the extra cash. More, she missed the bakery and her old customers. She would work a day or two a week in the bakery.

Heather and my former classmates had arrived as a group to help me celebrate the opening of my bakery. They were now placing their orders with Katie and Diana. After I greeted them all, Murray took my hand and led me to the door.

"Where are we going?" I asked. "I have customers to serve."

"Katie and Diana can handle things for now. You've been so busy the last few months. Take a moment to absorb what you've done."

Together we stepped out into the crisp fall air to admire the bakery-café. "You made this happen," Murray said. "That's got to feel good."

"Oh, I didn't do this by myself," I said. "You and so many other people helped me." I nodded at Katie and my friends in the bakery. "I couldn't have done this without you all."

"Isn't it amazing what you can do when you're willing to take a chance?"

"And when you have a plan," I said. My teacher, Heather, was right. Creating a business plan was the first step to starting any business. Once I had my business plan—my "recipe" for making a business—then it was just a matter of following that recipe step by step.

"I wonder where I would be now if I hadn't risked starting my own business," I said. "Likely still working at the donut shop in town, barely making ends meet."

"And the people living here would have no place to get together," Murray said. "You've given this community a gathering place."

Heather beckoned at me through the window to join my old classmates. Today I would celebrate all my hard work. I breathed in deeply, smelling the freshly baked cookies. Then, together with Murray, I stepped back inside.

Cookie's Oatmeal Doily Cookies

Doily cookies are also called lace or lacy cookies.

1 cup butter, left out to warm until it's soft
2 cups brown sugar, packed into the
  measuring cup
1 teaspoon vanilla
2 cups old fashioned rolled oats
¼ cup flour
pinch of salt

Use an electric mixer to blend the butter and sugar together in a bowl. Stir the vanilla into the mixture.

In another bowl, spoon together the rolled oats, flour and salt. Slowly add the oatmeal mixture to the butter and sugar, stirring as you go.

Chill the cookie dough in the fridge for an hour.

Remove the dough from the fridge, and heat the oven to 350° F.

Place a sheet of parchment paper on a baking sheet. Roll teaspoons of the dough into balls and place them on the parchment paper, leaving lots of room between balls. Press each ball flat. For added flavor, sprinkle each cookie with brown sugar before baking.

Pop the cookies into the oven and bake for about 10 minutes. But watch the cookies as they bake. They burn easily.

When the cookies are golden brown, take them out of the oven. Leave them on the baking sheet for a couple of minutes. Then put them onto a plate to cool fully. The cookies are so thin, they break easily, so be careful as you take them off the baking sheet.

For an added treat, serve the cookies with ice cream.

PREVIEW OF
NO RETURN ADDRESS BY
GAIL ANDERSON-DARGARTZ

That Saturday morning I woke feeling sad but didn't know why. The sun was shining. The lilac bushes in my front yard were in bloom. It was one of those June mornings that usually put a spring in my step. But this day my sadness deepened as the morning wore on.

I tried to shake the feeling by walking down to the village. I took in the cloudless blue sky over the mountains and breathed in the scent of the wild roses that grew along the rural road. But that didn't help.

By the time I reached the post office I felt real grief.

I must have looked sad too. As I pushed through the door the postmistress asked, "You okay, Rhonda? Something wrong?"

"I'm fine," I told Susan. "Just a little tired, I guess."

I dodged more questions by opening my mailbox. Then I sorted my mail at the small counter, putting most of it in the recycling bin. Other than bills and advertising flyers, I didn't get much mail any more. People sent emails instead, of course.

My mother used to send me letters though, even after I moved to this lakeside village where she lived. She said emails were impersonal, just words on a screen. Handwritten letters, on the other hand, were a gift. I didn't understand why she kept sending me letters when I lived just up the road. But now that Mom had passed away, I missed getting them.

As I thought of my mother's letters, I finally figured out why I felt so sad. It had been exactly one year since my mother died. My eyes stung as a new wave of grief washed over me. But I didn't want to cry in front of the postmistress. I wiped my eyes and tried to focus on sorting my mail.

Then I came across a delivery notice card. A package had arrived in the mail for me. That was strange. I hadn't ordered anything online.

My birthday wasn't until fall so I knew the parcel wasn't from my aunt. Every September my mother's sister, Auntie Lisa, sends me a small gift by mail, even though she lives in the area. My brother Doug also has a house close by, but I hadn't seen him since Mom's funeral. Mom had been the one to bring our family together, for Sunday dinner at her condo.

I handed the delivery notice card to the postmistress. Susan paused as she took it. "You sure you're okay?" she asked.

I shrugged. "I just realized it's one year today since my mother died."

"Oh, honey, I'm so sorry." Susan squeezed my hand. "I loved your mom! Meg was such a dear woman. We visited here just about every day."

In her final years, my mom had lived in a condo only a couple of blocks from the post office. After my marriage ended, I rented my house just up the road from her. I was glad I did. Mom often took care of my son when he was too young to stay at home alone. And when Mom got the news from her doctor that she had breast cancer, I was there to help her out. As I thought of those final years with my mother, I started to tear up again.

"You and your mom were very close, weren't you?" Susan asked me.

I nodded. "She was always there for me," I said.

"I know you were a big help to her when she was sick."

"She helped me through a rough time too," I said.

"Your divorce?"

I hesitated before answering. I imagined my mother had told Susan about that. Mom wasn't always discreet. She sometimes told strangers, like Susan, about my life. Mom had also stuck her nose in my business, giving me advice even though I was a grown woman. But after her death, I would have given anything to have one last chat with her. I often wished for her guidance now, especially her tips on parenting my son Cody.

"I don't know how I would have gotten through my divorce without her," I said. "She took care of Cody when I needed to deal with—" I stopped there. Now I was giving Susan too much information. I could see why my mother had befriended Susan, though. She *was* easy to talk to.

Susan waited a moment to see if I would

continue. When I didn't, she waved the delivery notice card. "I'll get your package," she said.

I took off my glasses and wiped my eyes as I waited. I was glad I was the only person in the post office. It had been a year since my mother's death. Why was I crying *now*?

"Here you go," said Susan. She set a small box on the counter in front of me.

"This can't be right," I said.

"Wrong address?" Susan asked.

"No, it's addressed to me. But this package is from my *mother*."

"That's impossible. Like you said, Meg has been gone a year." Susan peered at the box. "And why do you think it's from her? There's no return address."

I ran a finger along my own address written on the brown wrapping. "I would know my mother's handwriting anywhere," I said. I looked up at Susan. "Did she send this *before* her death? Could this package have been lost in the mail for that long?"

Susan scratched her head. "I suppose. Stranger things have happened. I once read about a letter that was delivered forty-five years after it was sent." She took a close look at the postmark. "But your package was mailed this week."

I felt a shock run through me. *Could* my mother have sent this parcel? Was she still alive? I shook my head at the foolish idea. When my mother passed away, I was right there holding her hand. "I don't understand," I said. "Who sent this?"

Susan shrugged. "I guess you'll have to open it to find out." She looked down at the box as if she wanted to find out too.

While I liked Susan, I didn't know her that well. I wasn't about to open the package in front of her. Who knew what was inside?

Still, I couldn't wait until I got home. I carried the box back to the counter by the mailboxes. There I used my keys to rip the tape on the box. I tore off the brown paper wrapper and opened the flaps. "Oh!" I cried, because I couldn't believe what I found inside.

Acknowledgments

I'm grateful to Mitch Krupp for helping me build my own home-based business and to Carmen Burt for answering my questions on administrative-assistant courses. My thanks also goes to my editor, Ruth Linka, and to Orca Book Publishers for their commitment to literacy through the Rapid Reads program. I'm proud to be a Rapid Reads author.

While the oatmeal doily cookie recipe at the end of the novel is my own, based on cookies my mother made, I also found inspiration from the lacy oatmeal cookie recipe found in *The New Basics Cookbook* by Julee Rosso and Sheila Lukins (Workman Publishing, New York) and from Maria Gray's YouTube video titled "Oatmeal Lace Cookies." I hope you enjoy making your own.

Author's Note

This short novel is intended to give the adult literacy learner a general sense of the steps involved in starting a small business. For specifics, a good starting place is the Canada Business Network (www.canadabusiness.ca) and the Community Futures Network of Canada (www.communityfuturescanada.ca). Also useful to me as I wrote this book was the guide *Start & Run A Home-Based Food Business*, by Mimi Shotland Fix (Self-Counsel Press, Vancouver). If this fiction writer can start a small business, you can too.

By the age of eighteen, **GAIL ANDERSON-DARGATZ** knew she wanted to write about women in rural settings. Today Gail is the author of several bestselling novels: *The Cure for Death by Lightning*, *A Recipe for Bees*, *A Rhinestone Button*, *Turtle Valley* and *The Spawning Grounds*. She has also written several short novels, like this one. Gail teaches other authors how to write fiction and divides her time between the Shuswap region of British Columbia and Manitoulin Island in Ontario. For more information, visit www.gailanderson-dargatz.ca or follow @AndersonDargatz.